'Twas the Night Before Christmas

Clement Clarke Moore

illustrated by

CHRISTOPHER WORMELL

Library of Congress Control Number: 2010924429
ISBN 978-0-7624-2717-8

Cover and interior design by: Frances J. Soo Ping Chow
Typography: Cavalcade, Chorus Girl,
ITC Berkeley, and Phaeton

Published by Running Press Kids,
an imprint of
Running Press Book Publishers
2300 Chestnut Street
Philadelphia, PA 19103-4371

Visit us on the web!
www.runningpress.com

For Daisy and Eliza

'Twas the Night Before Christmas

Clement Clarke Moore

illustrated by

CHRISTOPHER WORMELL

RP|KIDS
PHILADELPHIA · LONDON

'Twas the
NIGHT BEFORE
CHRISTMAS,
when all through the house

Not a creature was stirring,
NOT EVEN A MOUSE;

THE STOCKINGS WERE HUNG

by the chimney with care

In hopes that

ST. NICHOLAS

SOON WOULD BE THERE;

The Children were nestled
ALL SNUG IN THEIR BEDS,
While visions of sugar-plums
danced in their heads;

And mamma in her 'kerchief,
and I in my cap,

Had just settled our brains
FOR A LONG WINTER'S NAP,

When out on the lawn there arose
SUCH A CLATTER,

I sprang from the bed
to see what was the matter.

Away to the window
I FLEW LIKE A FLASH,

Tore open the shutters
and threw up the sash.

The moon on the breast of
THE NEW-FALLEN SNOW

Gave the lustre of mid-day to objects below,

When, what to my wondering eyes
should appear,

But a
MINIATURE SLEIGH,
AND EIGHT TINY REINDEER,

With a little old driver,
SO LIVELY AND QUICK,
I knew in a moment
IT MUST BE ST. NICK.

More rapid than eagles his coursers they came,
And he whistled, and shouted, and called them by name:

"NOW, DASHER! NOW, DANCER!
NOW, PRANCER
AND VIXEN!
ON, COMET! ON, CUPID!
ON, DONDER AND
BLITZEN!

To the top of the porch!
To the top of the wall!

NOW DASH AWAY! DASH AWAY!
DASH AWAY ALL!"

As dry leaves that before
the wild hurricane fly,

When they meet with an obstacle,
MOUNT TO THE SKY;

So up to the house-top
the coursers they flew,

With the sleigh
FULL OF TOYS,
AND ST. NICHOLAS TOO.

And then, in
A TWINKLING,
I heard on the roof
The prancing and pawing
OF EACH
LITTLE HOOF.

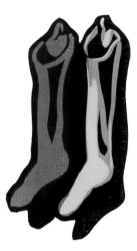

As I drew in my head,
and was turning around,

Down the chimney
ST. NICHOLAS CAME
WITH A BOUND.

He was dressed
ALL IN FUR,
from his head to his foot,

And his clothes were all tarnished
with ashes and soot;

A BUNDLE OF TOYS
he had flung on his back,

And he looked like
A PEDDLER JUST
OPENING HIS PACK.

His eyes—how they twinkled!
His dimples how merry!

HIS CHEEKS WERE LIKE ROSES,

his nose like a cherry!

His droll little mouth was drawn up

LIKE A BOW,

And the beard of his chin

WAS AS WHITE AS THE SNOW;

The stump of a pipe
he held tight in his teeth,

And the smoke
it encircled his head
like a wreath;

He had a broad face and
A LITTLE
ROUND BELLY,

That shook when he laughed,
like a bowlful of jelly.

He was chubby and plump,
A RIGHT JOLLY
OLD ELF,
And I laughed when I saw him,
in spite of myself;

A WINK OF HIS EYE
AND A TWIST OF HIS HEAD,
Soon gave me to know
I had nothing to dread;

He spoke not a word,
BUT WENT STRAIGHT
TO HIS WORK,
AND FILLED ALL THE STOCKINGS;
then turned with a jerk,

And laying his finger
ASIDE OF HIS NOSE,

And
GIVING A NOD,
UP THE CHIMNEY
HE ROSE;

HE SPRANG TO HIS SLEIGH,

to his team gave a whistle,

AND AWAY THEY ALL FLEW

like the down of
a thistle.

But I heard him exclaim,
ere he drove out of sight,

"HAPPY CHRISTMAS TO ALL,
AND TO ALL A GOOD-NIGHT."

'Twas the Night Before Christmas

and Clement Clarke Moore

'Twas the Night Before Christmas," originally titled "A Visit from St. Nicholas," was first published in the Troy, New York *Sentinel* on December 23, 1823. This classic poem has shaped our contemporary conception of Santa Claus with his rosy cheeks, sack of toys, and team of reindeer.

Twenty-one years after its first publication, Clement Clarke Moore claimed authorship when he published "'Twas The Night Before Christmas" in a book of poetry. He is credited as the author today, even though the anonymity of the original publication still leaves some doubtful. Some speculate that the original author is in fact Henry Livingston, but no substantial evidence exists to support this claim.

Clement Clarke Moore graduated from Columbia College and began his career as a professor of biblical study. His interest in ancient languages lead him to serve as a professor of Oriental and Greek literature at the General Theological Seminary, and, eventually, to write one of his greatest intellectual accomplishments, the two-volume *Compendious Lexicon of the Hebrew Language*. Moore claimed that he originally published "A Visit From St. Nicholas" anonymously because he considered it to be an embarrassment for a scholar to write such trivial material. However, he never anticipated that this "trivial" poem would become a worldwide Christmas tradition.